The People of the Town

Nursery~Rhyme Friends for You and Me

Selected and illustrated by
Alan Marks

iːi Charlesbridge

To my daughters, Charlotte and Lilly

The People of the Town presents poems that exist in many versions. Nursery rhymes change over time and vary by location.

Published by Charlesbridge • 85 Main Street, Watertown, MA 02472
(617) 926-0329 • www.charlesbridge.com

Library of Congress Cataloging-in-Publication Data
Marks, Alan, 1957– author, illustrator.
The people of the town: nursery-rhyme friends for you and me/Alan Marks.
pages cm
Summary: An illustrated collection of traditional and classic nursery rhymes.
ISBN 978-1-58089-726-6 (reinforced for library use)
ISBN 978-1-60734-967-9 (ebook)
ISBN 978-1-60734-968-6 (ebook pdf)
1. Nursery rhymes. 2. Children's poetry. [1. Nursery rhymes.] I. Mother Goose. II. Title.

PZ8.3.M39147Fr 2016
398.8—dc23
2015021181

Printed in China
(hc) 10 9 8 7 6 5 4 3 2 1

Illustrations done in pencil, ink, and watercolor on Daler Bloxworth paper
Display type set in Myster Bold by Denis Serebryakov
Text type set in Perpetua by Monotype
Color separations by Colourscan Print Co Pte Ltd, Singapore
Printed by 1010 Printing International Limited in Huizhou, Guangdong, China
Production supervision by Brian G. Walker
Designed by Diane M. Earley

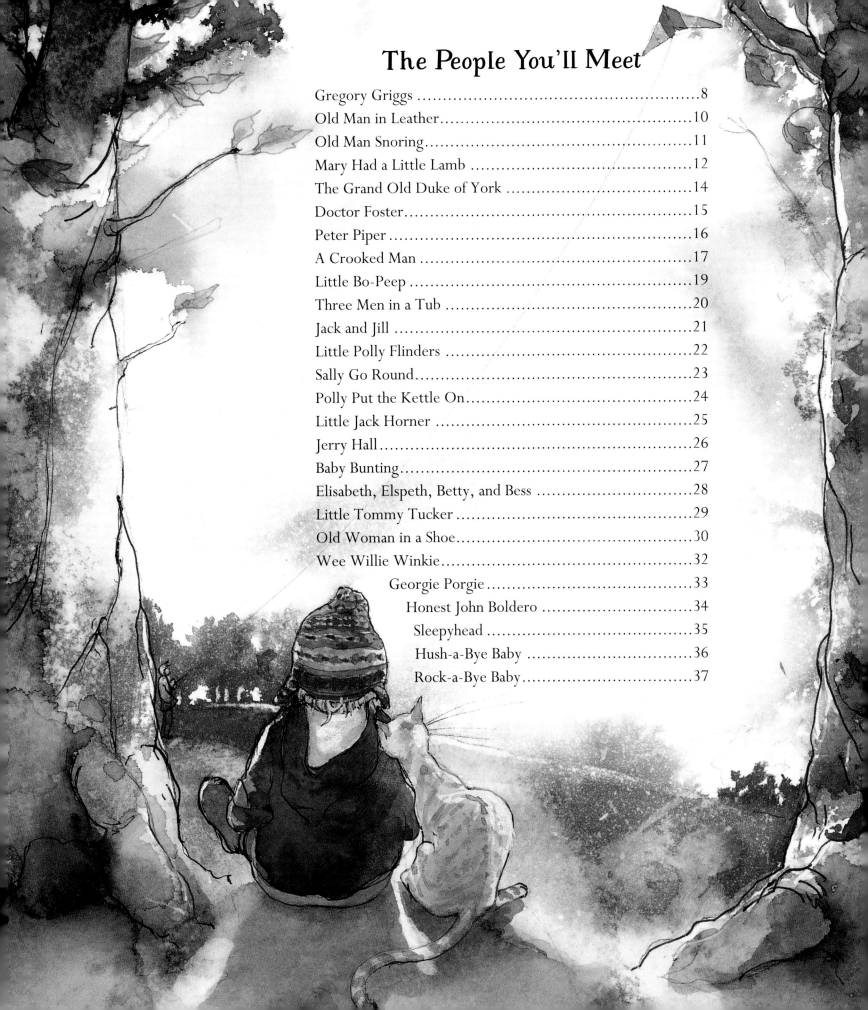

The People You'll Meet

Gregory Griggs, Gregory Griggs,
Had twenty-seven different wigs.
He wore them up, he wore them down,
To please the people of the town.
He wore them east, he wore them west,
But he could never tell which he loved the best.

9

One misty, moisty morning,
When cloudy was the weather,
There I met an old man
Clothed all in leather.

Clothed all in leather,
With a cap under his chin,
How do you do, and how do you do,
And how do you do again?

It's raining, it's pouring.
The old man is snoring.
He went to bed
And bumped his head
And couldn't get up in the morning.

Mary had a little lamb;
Its fleece was white as snow.
And everywhere that Mary went
The lamb was sure to go.

It followed her to school one day,
Which was against the rule;
It made the children laugh and play
To see a lamb at school.

And so the teacher turned it out,
But still it lingered near,
And waited patiently about
Till Mary did appear.

"Why does the lamb love Mary so?"
The eager children cry.
"Why, Mary loves the lamb, you know,"
The teacher did reply.

13

Oh,
The grand old Duke of York,
He had ten thousand men;
He marched them up to the top of the hill,
And he marched them down again.
And when they were up, they were up,
And when they were down, they were down,
And when they were only halfway up,
They were neither up nor down.

Doctor Foster went to Gloucester
In a shower of rain.
He stepped in a puddle,
Right up to his middle,
And never went there again!

Peter Piper picked a peck of pickled peppers.
A peck of pickled peppers Peter Piper picked.
If Peter Piper picked a peck of pickled peppers,
Where's the peck of pickled peppers Peter Piper picked?

There was a crooked man, and he walked a crooked mile.
He found a crooked sixpence upon a crooked stile.
He bought a crooked cat, which caught a crooked mouse,
And they all lived together in a little crooked house.

Little Bo-Peep has lost her sheep
And doesn't know where to find them;
Leave them alone, and they'll come home,
Bringing their tails behind them.

Little Bo-Peep fell fast asleep
And dreamt she heard them bleating;
But when she awoke, she found it a joke,
For they were still a-fleeting.

Then up she took her little crook,
Determined for to find them;
She found them indeed, but it made her heart bleed,
For they'd left their tails behind them.

It happened one day, as Bo-Peep did stray
Into a meadow hard by;
There she espied their tails side by side,
All hung on a tree to dry.

She heaved a sigh and wiped her eye,
And over the hillocks she raced,
And tried what she could, as a shepherdess should,
That each tail be properly placed.

Rub-a-dub-dub,
Three men in a tub,
And who do you think they be?
The butcher, the baker,
The candlestick maker—
Turn 'em out, knaves all three.

Jack and Jill went up the hill
To fetch a pail of water;
Jack fell down and broke his crown,
And Jill came tumbling after.

Then up Jack got and home did trot
As fast as he could caper;
And went to bed to mend his head
With vinegar and brown paper.

Little Polly Flinders
Sat among the cinders,
Warming her pretty little toes.
Her mother came and caught her
And scolded her little daughter
For spoiling her nice new clothes.

Sally go round the sun,
Sally go round the moon,
Sally go round the chimney pots
On a Saturday afternoon.

Polly put the kettle on,
Polly put the kettle on,
Polly put the kettle on,
We'll all have tea.

Sukey take it off again,
Sukey take it off again,
Sukey take it off again,
They've all gone away.

24

Little Jack Horner
Sat in a corner,
Eating a Christmas pie.
He put in his thumb
And pulled out a plum
And said, "What a good boy am I!"

Jerry Hall,
He is so small,
A rat could eat him,
Hat and all.

Bye, baby bunting,
Daddy's gone a-hunting,
Gone to get a little rabbit skin
To wrap the baby bunting in.

Elisabeth, Elspeth, Betty, and Bess,
All went together to seek a bird's nest.
They found a bird's nest with five eggs in.
They all took one and left four in.

Little Tommy Tucker
Sings for his supper.
What shall we give him
But white bread and butter?
How shall he cut it
Without a knife?
How shall he marry
Without a wife?

There was an old woman who lived in a shoe.
She had so many children she didn't know what to do.

She gave them some broth without any bread;
She kissed them all soundly and put them to bed.

Wee Willie Winkie runs through the town,
Upstairs and downstairs in his nightgown,
Tapping at the window and crying through the lock,
"Are all the children in their beds? It's past eight o'clock!"

Georgie Porgie, pudding and pie,
Kissed the girls and made them cry.
When the boys came out to play,
Georgie Porgie ran away.

To make your candles last for aye,
You wives and maids give ear-o.
To put them out's the only way,
Says honest John Boldero.

"To bed, to bed!"
Says Sleepyhead.
"Tarry awhile," says Slow.
"Put on the pan,"
Says greedy Nan,
"Let's sup before we go!"

Hush-a-bye, baby, on the tree-top,
When the wind blows, the cradle will rock;
When the bough breaks, the cradle will fall,
Down will come baby, cradle and all.

Rock-a-bye, baby,
Thy cradle is green;
Father's a nobleman,
Mother's a queen;
And Betty's a lady
And wears a gold ring;
And Johnny's a drummer
And drums for the king.